bee

butterflies

water

radish

onions

tomatoes

sunflower

daisies

basil

strawberries

snail

strawbe

tomato

A Peaceful GARDEN

Words by Lucy London • Illustrations by Christa Pierce

HARPER
An Imprint of HarperCollinsPublishers

For my dad. Thanks for our backyard
gardens and handmade chicken coops
and for letting me wash your truck
with my stuffed animals. —C.P.

A Peaceful Garden

Text copyright © 2018 by Lucy London • Illustrations copyright © 2018 by Christa Pierce

ISBN 978-0-06-229747-1
The artist used watercolor and Adobe Illustrator to create
the digital illustrations for this book.

Typography by Chelsea C. Donaldson

17 18 19 20 21 SCP 10 9 8 7 6 5 4 3 2 1
❖   First Edition

To grow a peaceful garden . . .
wait for the last frost
(just kiss the cold good-bye!),

dig yourself a patch

(soft soil is best—
no clumps!),

and check on the sun
(to make sure it's still there—your garden will need it!).

Do you have a
garden hat?

How about
a rake?

and a bucket
(for all the things you'll grow!).

A peaceful garden is for growing many things you might want to eat.

So, it's time to choose some seeds. . . .

Do you like carrots? (Big Tops are nice!)

Easy-peasy peas? (They'll need a wee pea fence.)

Lettuces are always lovely,
don't you think?

A peaceful garden is also for growing many things that others might want to eat.

Bees love daisies.

So do butterflies.

Would you like to invite some blackbirds?

Then plant an invitation:
sunflowers!

You can dig some small holes now.
And *plook-plook-plook* go the seeds.
Very nice. Little paws can tuck them in.

Don't forget what is where!

Small signs are good.

carrots

Now what?

Water! Gentle showers are best.

(You can give yourself one if you like.)

Water. Water. Water.
Every day (except the rainy ones).
Water is important for growing things.

You could also fill up
a little saucer for the bees.

(A few rocks will help them to not fall in.)

And a bath for the birds.
This will make your garden even more peaceful.

Especially in the mornings.

peas

lettuce

onions

radish

What a pretty patch you've made.
You've given your peaceful garden
everything it needs to grow.

peas

lettuce

onions

radish

carrots

Kale

And now you and the bees and the birds
and the rabbits can all wait together . . .

for your feast!